# EVERETT ANDERSON'S FRIEND

*by* LUCILLE CLIFTON      *Illustrations by* ANN GRIFALCONI

HENRY HOLT AND COMPANY • *New York*

Henry Holt and Company, LLC
*Publishers since 1866*
115 West 18th Street
New York, New York 10011

Henry Holt is a registered trademark
of Henry Holt and Company, LLC

Text copyright © 1976 by Lucille Clifton
Illustrations copyright © 1976 by Ann Grifalconi
All rights reserved.
Published in Canada by Fitzhenry & Whiteside Ltd.,
195 Allstate Parkway, Markham, Ontario L3R 4T8.
Library of Congress Cataloging-in-Publication Data
Clifton, Lucille.
Everett Anderson's friend / Lucille Clifton; illustrations by Ann Grifalconi.
Summary: Having eagerly anticipated the new neighbors, a boy is
disappointed to get a whole family of girls.
[1. Friendship—Fiction.  2. Stories in rhyme.]  I. Grifalconi, Ann, ill.  II. Title.
PZ8.3.C573Evg 1992 [E]—dc20  92-8030


ISBN 0-8050-2246-5
10  9  8  7  6  5  4  3  2

First published in hardcover in 1976 by Holt, Rinehart and Winston
Reissued in 1992 by Henry Holt and Company
Printed in Mexico

To Everett Anderson's Friends
—L. C.

To the Friends We Keep
—A. G.

Someone new has come to stay
in 13A, in 13A
and Everett Anderson's Mama and he
can't wait to see, can't wait to see
whether it's girls or
whether it's boys and
how are their books and
how are their toys and
where they've been and
where they go and
who are their friends and
the people they know,
oh, someone new has come to stay
next door in 13A.

If not an almost
brother,
why not something
other
like a bird or
a cat or
a cousin or
a dozen uncles?

Please,
says Everett Anderson softly,
why did they have to be
a family of
shes?

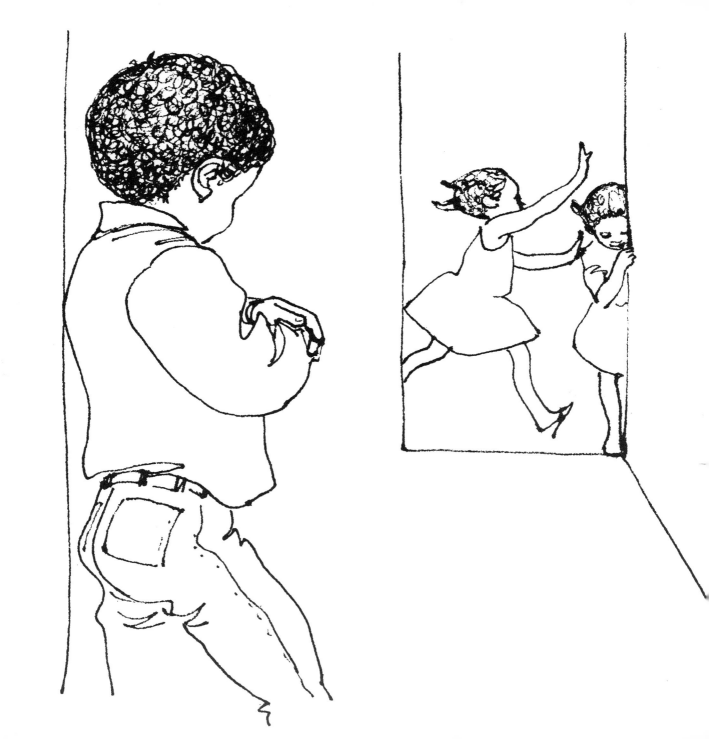

Girls named Maria who
win at ball
are not a bit of fun
at all.
No, girls who can run
are just no fun
thinks Everett Anderson!

In 14A when Mama's at work
sometimes Joe and sometimes Kirk
can come till she gets home and be
Everett Anderson's company.

Three boys are just the right amount
for playing games that count,
there isn't any room, you see,
for girls named Maria in company.

If Daddy was here
he would let me in and
call me a careless boy
and then
(even though I
 forgot my key)
he would make peanut butter
and jelly for me,
and not be mad
and I'd be glad.

If Daddy was here
he could let me in
thinks Everett Anderson
again.

A girl named Maria
is good to know
when you haven't got
any place to go
and you forgot your
apartment key.

Why, she can say,
"Come in with me,
 and play in 13A and wait
 if your Mama is working late."

Even if she beats at races it's
nicer to lose in familiar places.

Maria's Mama makes little pies
called *Tacos*,
calls little boys *Muchachos*,
and likes to thank the *Dios*;
oh, 13A is a lovely surprise
to Everett Anderson's eyes!

Everett Anderson's Mama is mad
because he lost the key he had;
but a boy has so many things to do
he can't remember them and keys, too.
And if Daddy were here he would say,
"We'll talk about it another day,"
thinks the boy who got a fussing at
for just a little thing like that.

A girl named Maria
who wins at ball
is fun to play with
after all
and Joe and Kirk and
Maria too
are just the right number
for things to do.

Lose a key,
win a friend,
things have a way of
balancing out,
Everett Anderson's Mama explains,
and that's what the world is all about.

And the friends we find
are full of surprises
Everett Anderson realizes.

## ABOUT THE AUTHOR AND ILLUSTRATOR

LUCILLE CLIFTON, poet, storyteller, college professor, mother of six and a grandmother, is the author of many books for young readers. Seven of her picture books with Henry Holt feature Everett Anderson, including *Everett Anderson's Goodbye* (a Coretta Scott King Award winner), *Everett Anderson's Nine Month Long,* and *Everett Anderson's Christmas Coming.*

Ms. Clifton lives in Maryland.

ANN GRIFALCONI, a native New Yorker, is the author and illustrator of *The Village of Round and Square Houses* and *Darkness and the Butterfly.* As an illustrator, she has collaborated with many writers on several picture books, including five Everett Anderson titles.

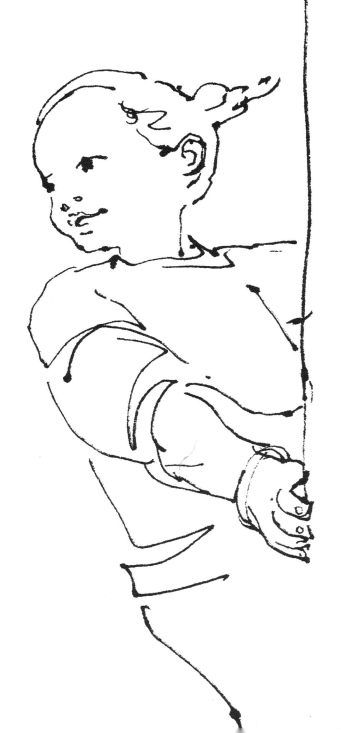

| 13A | 13A | 13A | 13A | 13 |
| 13A | 13A | 13A | 13A | 13 |
| 13A | 13A | 13A | 13A | 13 |
| 13A | 13A | 13A | 13A | 13 |
| 13A | 13A | 13A | 13A | 13 |
| 13A | 13A | 13A | 13A | 13 |